Albidaro
AND THE
Mischievous
Dream

✱

JULIUS LESTER
JERRY PINKNEY

PHYLLIS FOGELMAN BOOKS

NEW PF **YORK**

One day children got tired of having to do what their parents told them.

"Time to get up," parents said when children were sound asleep.

"Time to go to bed," parents said when children were wide awake.

"Don't eat so much," parents said when children were eating something they liked.

"Eat some more," parents said when it was something children didn't like.

Parents did not make sense and children were tired of it. But what could they do?

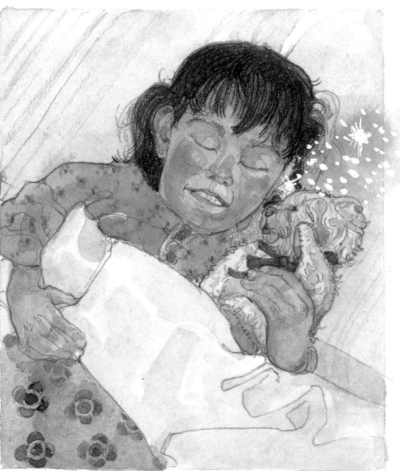

Better than anything and anybody in the world, teddy bears know how children feel. So one night when the children were sleeping a sleep as sweet as flower juice, their teddy bears gave the children a dream as happy as a butterfly's heart. The children started laughing in their sleep as the dream told them what to do when they woke up the next morning.

But then something strange happened. Even the teddy bears were surprised, and everybody knows how hard it is to surprise a teddy bear!

The dream said, "I'm so wonderful! I think I'll also give myself to the children who don't have teddy bears. Yes! I'll give myself to all the children in all the world!"

"Oh, no! Don't do that!" the teddy bears said to the dream in voices as small as bees' eyes. But it was too late.

Quieter than darkness and faster than fear, the dream was already going from child to child, telling them that when they awoke, they could do whatever they wanted, when they wanted, and they would *never* be punished.

One day children got tired of having to do what their parents told them.

"Time to get up," parents said when children were sound asleep.

"Time to go to bed," parents said when children were wide awake.

"Don't eat so much," parents said when children were eating something they liked.

"Eat some more," parents said when it was something children didn't like.

Parents did not make sense and children were tired of it. But what could they do?

Now, high in the mountains of Africa lived Albidaro, the Guardian of Children. From the beginning of time he had watched children while they slept to be sure no harm came to them. He could also hear the thoughts of teddy bears and see the dreams of children. So he chuckled while watching this dream weave itself into each child's heart. What fun his children would have if they didn't have to do what adults told them to. It would only be for a day or so. What harm could come from that?

Then he had an idea! His sister, Olara, was the Guardian of Animals and didn't care about anything or anyone except her animals. She never paid attention when he wanted her to look at his children taking their first steps or to see how proud they were on their first day of school.

Morning came. "Time to get up!" mothers and fathers all over the world called to their children.

"*Nyet,*" answered the children in Russia.

"*Lo,*" answered the children in Israel.

"*Non,*" answered the children in France.

"*Nein,*" answered the children in Germany.

"No," answered the children in Italy, South America, and Canada.

"Uh-uh," answered the children in the United States.

In every country on every continent, in every language that slipped off the tongue, the children would not get out of bed.

"What's the matter?" fathers and mothers wanted to know.

"From now on, we're going to do what WE want to do," the children answered. "And WE do not want to go to school today, and you can't make us!"

The parents were furious! They were so furious that their anger would have swallowed the children if something hadn't scared it. What happened so frightened the children, they forgot about doing what they wanted and ran to their parents. But the teddy bears were not surprised. *"We knew this was going to happen!"* they said in voices as soft as dragonfly tears.

What happened was that all the pets and all the animals in all the bedrooms and all the pet shops in all the world took off their leashes, unlocked their cages, and pushed the covers off their tanks. Canaries, mynah birds, parrots, monkeys, gerbils, dogs, rabbits, snakes, spiders, turtles, and fish crawled, ran, flew, slithered, and crept outside. Out of the jungles, forests, and mountains came lions, tigers, elephants, gorillas, chimps, water buffalo, hippopotamussesesssss, rhinossyhorses, and giraffes. They went to the airports, got on jet planes, and flew to Paris, New York, Shanghai, Cairo, Lima, Nairobi, and all the cities in the world.

"That elephant is out of its element," a mother in Stockholm said of the one lying in her son's bed.

"There's a tiger drinking cider with my daughter," said a father in Fargo.

"That llama is wearing my pajamas," exclaimed a father in Tokyo.

"That bear has my comb in his hair!" shouted a grandmother in Manila.

Snakes were curled on couches watching videos and eating popcorn while dogs played baseball, buzzards rode bicycles, buffalo jumped rope, penguins surfed the Internet, and whales played soccer. But the animals had the most fun dressing up in the parents' best clothes and going out to fancy restaurants.

Back on a mountaintop in Africa a woman as beautifully black as a panther on a night when there was no moon watched her animals and could not understand why they were acting like . . . like *people*. Why would they suddenly want to be so silly?

"Albidaro?" Olara called to her brother. "What is going on? Help me! Please!"

"My goodness!" Albidaro exclaimed, pretending to be surprised. "Your animals look so foolish. Did you do something to them?"

"Don't be ridiculous!" Olara shot back. "And you'd better wipe that smirk off your face. It doesn't seem to me that your children are very happy!" She was right. The children did not like having to share their homes with the animals.

"Turn the water off," a child told a giraffe when it came out of the shower.

The giraffe looked at the child and wandered away, dripping water all over the house.

"Come help me put the dishes in the dishwasher," another child said to a rhinossyhorse. The rhinossyhorse sat on the dishwasher and squashed it, breaking all the dishes and pots and silverware inside.

The children went to their parents. "Mom? Dad? Please make things like they were before."

"We wish we could," the mothers and fathers said, "but the animals won't listen to us either."

The children went and sat in corners and began to cry.

High on the mountain in Africa Albidaro started to cry too. This was not what he had thought would happen. He should have learned by now that teddy bears are always right!

Albidaro knew he had to tell Olara that it was his fault, that he had been playing a joke on her. "I'm sorry," he concluded. "Can you make the animals be animals again so my children will stop crying?"

Olara was angry with her brother, but before she could say anything, out of the corner of her eye she saw some animals on skateboards and Rollerblades, and some monkeys playing golf.

Olara swooped down. "What do you think you're doing?" she asked the monkeys, her voice trembling with rage.

"Trying to make this par three, if you'll be quiet," one monkey replied.

"That's it!" Olara exclaimed. "Let's see how you really like being different."

Olara flew high into the navel of the sky and clapped her hands three times. Suddenly giraffes had short legs; lions were bald, and when they went to roar, only a squeak came out. Dogs meowed, cats barked, and elephants became the size of bugs. Tigers were pink with green stripes, and monkeys were as yellow as bananas. Whales had wheels, and birds swam.

The animals looked at each other and remembered how noble and beautiful they had been once. They raised their faces and looked up at Olara hovering high in the heavens above them.

"We're sorry," the dogs meowed.

"We're sorry," the cats barked.

"We're sorry," the lions and tigers squeaked.

Satisfied with their apologies, Olara clapped her hands again and the animals went back to their cages and tanks, back to the jungles and mountains where they were supposed to be, looking like they were supposed to look and sounding like they were supposed to sound.

Then Albidaro put all the people into a deep sleep. When they awoke the next morning, no one remembered what had happened.

No one, that is, except the teddy bears.

Olara told them that if they ever told anyone what had happened, she would turn them into Brussels sprouts. And no child would cuddle with a Brussels sprout.

Well, teddy bears like to cuddle more than anybody in the world, so they promised not to say a word—ever.

And that's why, to this day, teddy bears look like they have a secret.

To Milan,
My dream come true
J. L.

For my grandchildren,
Gloria, Myles, Charnelle, Victoria, Rashad,
Rian, Chloe, and Dobbin
J. P.

Published by Phyllis Fogelman Books
An imprint of Penguin Putnam Books for Young Readers
345 Hudson Street
New York, New York 10014

Text copyright © 2000 by Julius Lester
Pictures copyright © 2000 by Jerry Pinkney
All rights reserved
Designed by Atha Tehon
Text set in Hiroshige
Printed in Hong Kong on acid-free paper
1 3 5 7 9 10 8 6 4 2

Library of Congress Cataloging-in-Publication Data
available upon request

The full-color artwork has been prepared
using pencil, gouache, and watercolor on paper.